Love Waves

ROSEMARY WELLS

CANDLEWICK PRESS

❧ Mama Goes to Work ❧

Be brave.

As I leave, I see you wave.
I have to go where I must be,

serving cookies, cakes, and tea.

Soon I wonder where you are:

Zooming in your racing car?
Swinging high above the trees?
Eating honey with your peas?

Is that you at the window
on the street?

No. Someone else,
racing off on someone else's feet.

I bring a coffee with éclair,
then send you love waves
through the air.

Around the world, around the sun,
they fly a thousand miles or one.

Nothing stops them on their way.

"I'm coming home!"
the love waves say.

Listen for my turning key.
Find our chair and wait for me.

Daddy Goes to Work

Kiss me.

Tell me that you'll miss me.
I will miss you more.

I must go down in the subway train,
then up to the highest floor.

Ring! Ring! goes my telephone.
Could it please be you?

Are you trying to button your shirt?
Can you tie your shoe?

Out my office window, can you hear me sing,

over the noise of the city,
the song of the Pirate King?

I send love waves speeding,
flying as fast as birds,
catching rides in taxis . . .

silvery ribbons of words:
"Daddy is coming. He's on his way."

Tell me
all about your day.

When we are far away
or only down the hall,

we will send you love waves,
let them fall . . .

like twinkles on your pillow
and in your sleeping hand,
spilling over the hills of bed,
warm as island sand.

And in your dream,
mysterious as Mars,
you'll send the love waves
back like shooting stars.

To Frances

love wave: The externalized product of affection so vibrant and ample that it cannot be contained by a single heart alone and can, therefore, be shared with a loved one anywhere through the medium of thought, will, or wish. Similar to radio waves; invisible and capable of being transmitted over great distances and through any obstacle.

Copyright © 2011 by Rosemary Wells

First edition in this format 2012

The Library of Congress has cataloged the original hardcover edition as follows:

Wells, Rosemary.
Love waves / Rosemary Wells. — 1st ed.
p. cm.
Summary: While they are at work a mother and father send powerful "love waves"
to their child at home, offering reassurance and comfort in their absence.
ISBN 978-0-7636-4989-0 (first edition)
[1. Separation anxiety — Fiction. 2. Parent and child — Fiction. 3. Love — Fiction.]   I. Title.
PZ8.3.W465Lo 2011
[E] — dc22   2010040460

ISBN 978-0-7636-6224-0 (midi edition)

12 13 14 15 16 17 SCP 10 9 8 7 6 5 4 3 2 1

Printed in Humen, Dongguan, China

This book was typeset in Quercus.
The illustrations were done in pastel.

Candlewick Press
99 Dover Street
Somerville, Massachusetts 02144

visit us at www.candlewick.com